COME BACK, DUSTY

MO

BUZZ

SNICKER

WACK

BACH

FARMER FI

WHEEZY

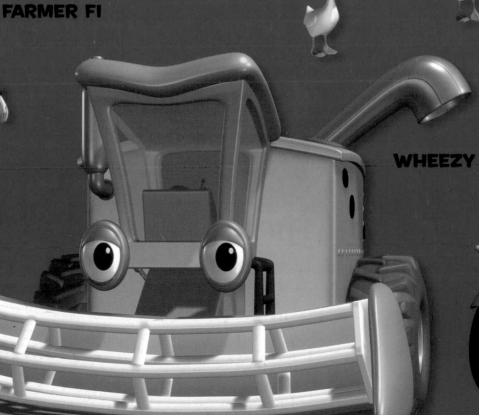

RORA

DUSTY

THE HENS

PURDEY

REV

RIFF

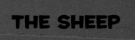

THE SHEEP

MATT

WINNIE

TOM

First published in Great Britain by
HarperCollins Children's Books in 2005

1 3 5 7 9 10 8 6 4 2

ISBN: 0-00-719933-3

Text adapted from the original script by Andrew Brenner

48 Margaret Street London W1W 8SE

www.contendergroup.com

Tractor Tom © Contender Ltd 2002

A CIP catalogue record for this title is available from the British Library.

Printed and bound in China

COME BACK, DUSTY

HarperCollins *Children's Books*

It was a busy day on Springhill Farm.
Everybody had a job to do.
   Tom and Buzz were stacking the hay bales
and Dusty and Farmer Fi were putting fertiliser
on the crops.

   "I wish I could fly like Dusty,"
sighed Buzz.
   "Let's go meet her, Buzz,"
cried Tom. "She's
coming in to land!"

Fi jumped out of Dusty and said hello to Tom
and Buzz.

"I'll just go and get things ready for your bath,
Dusty," Fi called, as she left.

Dusty didn't look very happy. She didn't like
having baths because she was worried about
getting soap in her eyes.

"Can you tell Fi I don't want a bath, Tom?
Please!" begged Dusty.

Matt and Rev also had an important job to do. They were on their way to pick up some manure from the stables and deliver it to Mr Aziz for his roses.

"Come on, Rev!" said Matt. "We've got a job to do."

"Yeah. A *smelly* job!" moaned Rev. He really didn't want to carry the stinky manure.

"This water isn't for you, it's for Dusty." said Fi.
Wack and Bach were having fun splishing and
splashing in Dusty's bath.

Just then Tom and Buzz came into the yard.
They told Fi that Dusty didn't want a bath.
But Fi said *everybody* had to stay clean and
she sent Tom and Buzz back to fetch Dusty.

So Tom and Buzz went off to tell Dusty.

"Sorry, Dusty. Fi says you have to have a bath. I'm sure she won't get soap in your eyes," said Tom, kindly.

But Dusty had other ideas.

"You'll have to catch me first!" she shouted, and flew off.

Back at the stables Matt was busy collecting
the manure from Winnie and Snicker's stall.

"Phew, this really is *smelly* work," said Matt.

"That's why I wanted someone else to do it,"
grumbled Rev.

Rev didn't like the idea of having to carry
lots of smelly manure. So when Matt wasn't
looking, naughty Rev ran off to help Tom and
Buzz catch Dusty.

Dusty had landed in the field next to Mo.

"I wish I were a cow, like you, Mo. You don't have baths, do you?" said Dusty.

"Moo!" nodded Mo.

"You do?" said Dusty, surprised.

Suddenly, Dusty spotted Tom, Rev, and Buzz racing towards her. Dusty quickly took off.

"Come back, Dusty!" shouted Tom.
But Dusty
just laughed.

Rev, Tom and Buzz rushed off after Dusty.

Bang! Silly Buzz hit a tree. He had been too busy looking up at Dusty to see where he was going.

Crash! Rev hit Matt's caravan. Smoke was pouring out of his engine.

A bit of smoke wasn't going to stop Rev though. Very soon he and Buzz and Tom were chasing after Dusty again.

The friends were in the next field when they
heard a loud *beeep!* It was Matt on Rora.
He had come to take naughty Rev back to finish
his job.

Rora said she
would stay and
help chase Dusty.

"We are never going to catch Dusty," said Buzz.
"When she sees us coming she just flies away."
Suddenly, Tom's light began to flash. He had
had an idea!

Tom put three bales of
hay on his forks and
hid behind them. Rora
and Buzz hid behind Tom.

Very quietly they crept up behind Dusty.

Every time Dusty turned around Rora, Tom
and Buzz stopped. As soon as they were
close to Dusty, they all leapt out from behind
the hay bales!
But Dusty was too quick for them.
She soared off.

Putt, putt!

Oh, no! That noise meant Dusty was out of fuel. And she was heading straight for Mo!

Quickly, Tom lifted Mo up in his forks. He scooted out of the way just in time. Dusty landed safely.

Tom, Rora, and Buzz told Dusty she shouldn't be afraid of having a bath. She agreed to go back to the farmyard.

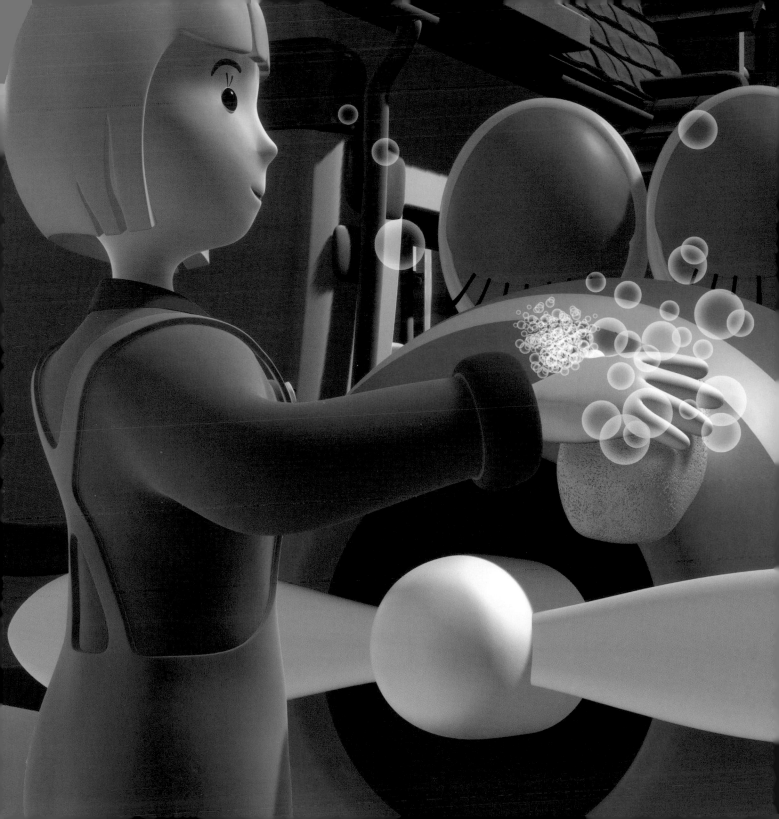

Fi gave Dusty her bath. She was careful not to get any soap in Dusty's eyes. Dusty kept her eyes shut tight, just in case.

"Having a bath wasn't so bad after all!" said Dusty, happily.

But Rev wasn't happy. He still had to take the manure to Mr Aziz. Phew! Rev was going to need a bath next!

MO

BUZZ

SNICKER

FARMER FI

WACK

BACH

WHEEZY

RORA

DUSTY

THE HENS

PURDEY

REV

RIFF

THE SHEEP

TOM

WINNIE

MATT

YOU CAN COLLECT THEM ALL!

1-84357-066-1 £3.99 — TRACTOR TOM'S **ACTIVITY BOOK**

1-84357-064-5 £3.99 — TRACTOR TOM AND THE **MOBILE PHONE**

1-84357-065-3 £3.99 — TRACTOR TOM'S "WHERE'S IT GONE?" **STICKER BOOK**

1-84357-087-4 £3.99 — TRACTOR TOM'S **SPORTS DAY**

0-00-718904-4 £5.99 — MY TRACTOR TOM PLAYBOOK — FIND AND FIT THE SHAPES TO HELP TRACTOR TOM ON THE FARM!

0-00-718900-1 £3.99 — **TREASURE TRAIL**

0-00-718901-X £3.99 — **A SURPRISE FOR FI**

0-00-718902-8 £3.99 — **BAA BAA TOM SHEEP**

0-00-718903-6 £3.99 — **A JOB FOR BUZZ**

WHAT WOULD WE DO WITHOUT HIM?